Lily

Patricia Polacco

G. P. PUTNAM'S SONS   An Imprint of Penguin Group (USA) Inc.

It was the first day at my new school. I lived right across the bay from the Golden Gate Bridge now, and it was beautiful to look at, but it wasn't home yet, and I dreaded going to school. I missed my old school—and all my friends. My stomach was churning and my heart was pounding out of my chest.

When I made my way down the hall on my first day of school, everyone was rushing by me, talking and laughing. They all knew each other. I felt so alone.

"Hey!" a friendly voice called out. "You look how I feel! Are you new here, too?" a short round boy with rosy cheeks and a big smile asked.

I nodded.

"Me too! The name's Jamie . . . Jamie Aldrich," he chirped.

"I'm Lyla . . . Lyla Dean," I answered.

"So what grade are you in, anyway?" Jamie asked.

"Sixth," I answered.

"Me too! Bet we end up in the same homeroom," he said with a grin.

And he was right. Not only were we in the same homeroom, we sat right next to each other.

It didn't take very long for Jamie and me to become fast friends. We ate lunch together every day and watched the other kids break into groups. The kids they called "the geeks and the nerds" sat at one table, the "toughs" sat with other tough kids, skateboarders sat at their own table, arty kids at another. The sports kids had two tables and were the loudest!

Then there was the table where Gage, Kenyon and Maeve sat. They were the three most popular girls in the school, and they knew it. I learned soon enough that everyone wanted to be like them: they dressed like them, talked like them, even carried colored cell phones just like they did.

They called their table "the celebrity table."

One day on a school trip, I said to Jamie, "Everybody seems to have a cell phone."

"Pretty much." Jamie pulled his own cell phone out of his pocket. "You should get one, Lyla," he said. "And a laptop."

I shrugged. My father was a doctor and felt that cell phones were for emergencies, and the school had computers.

"You need to get both, Lyla . . . that's how you stay connected with the world! Get a Facebook page, too. I have one," he said enthusiastically.

It turned out Jamie was a computer nut! He knew everything there was to know about computers, and he promised to set me up if I could convince my parents to give me a cell phone and laptop.

As the weeks passed, I got to know a lot of other kids at school, and I liked them a lot. Jamie, by far, was my best buddy. It wasn't as if I had a crush on him or anything like that . . . but we were best friends for sure.

Gage, Kenyon and Maeve fascinated me even though they completely ignored me. That is, until I got the highest grade on a social studies essay. Mr. Rosen held up my paper and told the class how good it was. Gage gave me a really strange look and whispered, "I always get the best grades in this class." Then she winked and smiled.

It made me feel very uneasy.

When I told Jamie about what Gage said, he told me that Gage
had lost her parents in a terrible auto accident last year.

"That would be horrible to lose your parents," I said thoughtfully.

"Yeah, but she seems to milk it for all it's worth! Most kids are afraid
of her. You really need to be careful around her, Lyla."

A week later, I told Jamie I was going out for cheerleading. He warned
me again. "That's Gage, Maeve and Kenyon's territory, Lyla. Be careful!"

When I did the tryout routine the next day, I ended with a double flip and a split. It wasn't in the routine, but I had taken gymnastics since I was seven. I knew that I had nailed it. I thought my big ending would give me an edge.

I guess I was right, because when they read the names of the four new cheerleaders, they read mine first. Gage, Kenyon and Maeve actually smiled at me!

At dinner that night my brother Jack wasn't as excited as I had hoped he would be for me. Maybe because he had been having a hard time at his new school. Small for his age, he looked even younger. Kids were knocking his books out of his arms and calling him "sissy boy" or "doll-baby wimp." That kind of thing.

It seemed like a good time to tell my parents about the cell phones and laptops at school: "Everybody has their own!" I told them. "Maybe having them would help Jack and me get connected!"

Jack perked up. "That's true! When you have a cell and laptop, you're in the loop."

"And everyone has a Facebook page, too," I added excitedly. "Oh, please. . . ."

Mom and Dad looked at each other and thought for a moment.

Finally, they agreed. We cheered.

"But no shenanigans," Dad said. "The minute we hear that you are using these things inappropriately, you'll lose the privilege of having them."

Jamie helped Jack and me put our Facebook pages together.
He took our pictures and made us sound amazing.

At school Jamie was doing better, too. He even became a hall officer.
That meant that he went around to classrooms and collected attendance
slips. Then he'd bring them back to the office and record them. He was
really trusted. The principal, Mr. August, even let him go into the locked
room where all of the state tests were kept to get attendance forms.
That office was locked up like Fort Knox!

"Do you ever get to see the state tests?" I asked him one day.

"Noooooo. They are in sealed envelopes! The first time anyone
sees them is in February when we open them to take the test."

I was so proud to have someone like Jamie as a friend.

Gage, Maeve and Kenyon were actually starting to be nice to me. I wasn't good enough to sit at the celebrity table, though, until the Mid-Year Awards Assembly. The principal announced that I had the highest grade point average in the whole school, that I got a Junior Achievement Award for heading up a project visiting the elderly, and that I got the Spirit Award for cheerleading.

Gage usually got this award, but she seemed really happy that I got it. That's when she invited me to sit with them at the celebrity table at lunch.

Jamie was disappointed that I wouldn't be sitting with him, but understood that this was a "girl thing."

"Just as long as we still watch science fiction movies on Friday nights together," he said with a broad smile.

But before I got to sit at the table—in fact, that very night—Gage invited me over to her house for a makeover. I had to look "way cool," she said.

I went, and I did!

Every eye in the cafeteria was on me at the next lunch. I was sitting with the coolest girls in school. Gage, Kenyon and Maeve chatted about clothes, makeup—and boys. Then she leaned in to me.

"Let's get our mothers to take us to the mall tonight—we can look at clothes, maybe even eat at the Ground Cow!"

"I'd love to," I blurted out. I couldn't believe my luck.

Then I realized that was when Jamie and I watched our sci-fi together. As we got up and walked by his table, he smiled at me. "See you tonight."

Gage hissed, "Are you telling me that you are still friends with that?"

"OMG, he is such a blimp!" Kenyon spat out. They all laughed.

After that, I found myself pretending I didn't see Jamie. I still liked him a lot, we still had most of our movie nights, but I was torn.

He became my secret from them.

The rest of fall was great with Gage, Kenyon and Maeve. They picked out makeup for me and picked out my clothes. I loved it, and loved being with them. I wanted so much to be popular.

Then one day when we were at Gage's house, trying on some new makeup, Gage opened up her laptop. "We are going to do something a lot more fun."

She got a look on her face. "We call this scum dumping!" she said, and laughed. She started surfing through the Facebook pages of our classmates.

"Oh, look, here's Imogene O'Neal's page. Look at that picture! Those teeth!" Gage chided.

"She looks just like a horse," Maeve chimed in. They all laughed.

"And I've got just the right comment!" On Imogene's wall, I watched Gage post: "You look like a horse and sound like one, too." On Judy Marx's page

she wrote, "I hear your mother is chasing after the soccer coach. What would your daddy say?" On Audrey Jones's she wrote, "Your brother wears makeup and dresses when he's home alone."

All I could think of was how all of this would make me—or Jack or Jamie—feel, to see stuff like this on our Facebook walls.

They went onto five or six more pages of school friends, making comments. But then they came to Jamie's. "Oh, look, Pudding Butt has a Facebook page," Maeve sneered. Then they found a photo of a huge hippo and put Jamie's face on it. No comment necessary. I didn't say anything.

I knew I was letting Jamie down.

Having a laptop and cell did not help my brother! He was getting really mean messages like these almost daily. I didn't know how to help him. And a day later, on our Friday night, I asked Jamie.

"Jamie, why do people gang up on each other?"

Jamie shrugged. "You should see some of my messages."

My face flushed.

"I guess some people aren't happy unless they are putting someone else down, trashing them," he said softly.

He knew. I began to sob.

From that time on, I spent less and less time with Gage, Kenyon and Maeve.

I sat with Jamie at lunch the next Monday.

When Gage saw me, she cooed, "Did I see you sitting with Jamie Aldrich at lunch today? If you like Jamie so much, why don't you have him sit with us at the celebrity table? He'd be like a court jester . . . or a fat little clown."

I got up all the courage I could and pulled away from her. "Jamie Aldrich is no court jester, no clown, Gage. . . . And he's one of my best friends." I wanted to say, You and your friends are nothing but bullies. Bullies!

Even so, I walked away feeling like a ten-thousand-pound weight was off my shoulders. I was walking on air.

"No one dumps us, Lyla. We do the dumping!" Gage called after me.

Then the week of the state tests arrived. I just didn't know how to study for them—they covered everything we'd learned in the fall. And more. The day of the tests, everyone had to turn in their cell phones at the office. We also had to put our laptops, if we had one, in our lockers. Jamie sat right next to me in the test room. Gage, Maeve and Kenyon were on the other side of the room. It was a timed test that took over an hour.

When we finished, I sat with Jamie at lunch. Gage, Maeve and Kenyon strolled by me. They smiled and seemed really friendly.

A week later, the test scores were posted. I got the highest score on the test—99.6 percent.

That felt so good. Jamie did real well, too—99 percent. I noticed that Gage was third, not bad—97.

But later that same day, it was announced that the state test had been "compromised." One of the tests had been taken from the ward room before test day. That meant someone could have cheated. Since I got the highest score, I was the first one called into the office.

"Lyla," the principal started, "your teachers have informed me that you consistently make high test scores, but I have to ask you," he fumbled around, "did you take that test from the ward room?"

"Noooooo, Mr. August. I would never do that." I started to get tears in my eyes. "Never." Mr. August believed me and let me go.

Gage was right outside the door when I came out. Why, I didn't know. "Lyla," she whispered. "None of us believes that you had anything to do with the stolen test. We know you wouldn't do that." I wanted to gag!

By the time I got home that night, I was all over Facebook, MySpace, YouTube, and the school home page. All the tests were going to be thrown out, and everyone blamed me. I had hundreds of messages on my cell phone, and when I started to read them, I was stunned. Everyone was accusing me of stealing the test. And there were really horrible messages calling me names. "Phony!" "Cheater!" "Scagg!"

On Facebook, someone had changed my profile name to "Lying Lyla!"

The next day, everyone either gave me looks in the hall or walked on by as if I wasn't there at all. In one classroom, someone threw chewed gum at me. And Jamie was out of town—his grandmother in Rhode Island had died. I missed him terribly.

Mr. August called me and my parents into his office two days later.

Teachers were doubting my honesty, he said. In fact, they questioned
all of the work I had done all year.

"Surely, Mr. August, you don't believe those rumors, do you?"
My mother looked like she was about to cry.

I shook my head and whispered, "I know who did it, it's Gage,
I don't know how but I know it's Gage."

"Gage Lundon? Oh, Lyla, she lost her parents in that terrible accident.
Are you saying she has some part in this? Someone who has suffered
as she has? I find that hard to believe. Why, she is one of the few other
kids defending you!"

In my heart, I knew Gage was behind all of this. But now I knew
no one would believe me.

My life was miserable. No one at school would talk to me. It was as if I wasn't even there. Kids started throwing things at me when I was cheering and there were more and more horrible messages on my cell phone and on my Facebook wall.

When Jamie got home—finally!—I told him everything. But he just sat and watched me cry. Then he got a strange look on his face.

"Lyla . . . I think I can help you. Just sit tight!" Then he left.

The next morning, Mom and Dad got a call from Mr. August asking us all to come in for another meeting. When we got there, he almost couldn't look at me or my parents.

"Lyla," he began, "I want to offer you a profound apology for what you and your family have endured." He took a deep breath.

"It appears that another person stole the test, then launched a campaign on the Web and cell phones to see that you were blamed."

"But who was it, Mr. August? Who could do such a mean-spirited thing?" My mom was all teary.

"The person is a minor and I can't say. Just believe the matter is being handled," Mr. August answered.

"How did you discover the truth?" my father asked.

"A student came forward that saw the theft." He looked at me. "It cleared you, Lyla, completely."

I saw Jamie that night—it was a Friday. I could hardly wait.

"Jamie . . . someone saw who stole the test!"

Jamie smiled. "I know, Lyla . . . it was me. I was in the ward room getting attendance slips and saw Gage slip in! I must have left the door open or she was watching me. Anyway, she was in and out so fast, I didn't think anything of it. Then.

"But it was when I came back from Grandma's funeral, and you told me the trouble you were in, that I began to put two and two together. I still wasn't sure, but I told Mr. August and I showed him how to trace the messages."

"Oh, Jamie. You saved my life." I hugged him.

"Tracing the messages to her proved that Gage started the whole thing," Jamie said proudly.

He really was my best friend.

A lot of things happened after that. No more cell phones in class, laptops only for studying. But the kids didn't suddenly love me again.

"Nothing is going to change," Jack said. "Everybody will just go underground. What about when school isn't in session? No one can stop kids from using their cell phones and laptops."

To avoid suspension, Gage had to publicly admit what she did. She had to apologize on her cell phone and Facebook, too. But, somehow, I feared her apology would be lame. We'll see. She could still convince everyone that she was forced into being humiliated by me . . . and Jamie.

I had heard of a scapegoat before; now I knew what it was to be one. Jamie says that pathetic kids like Gage will always be looking for someone to go after.

My dad said, "Think about it, Lyla: in order for people like Gage's candle to glow brighter, she has to blow out yours."

But I have a decision to make. Should Jamie and I go back to school, hope for the best? Or should we go to another?

What would you do?

PATRICIA LEE GAUCH, EDITOR

G. P. Putnam's Sons
A division of Penguin Young Readers Group.
Published by The Penguin Group.
Penguin Group (USA) Inc., 375 Hudson Street, New York, NY 10014, U.S.A.
Penguin Group (Canada), 90 Eglinton Avenue East, Suite 700, Toronto, Ontario M4P 2Y3, Canada
(a division of Pearson Penguin Canada Inc.). Penguin Books Ltd, 80 Strand, London WC2R 0RL, England.
Penguin Ireland, 25 St. Stephen's Green, Dublin 2, Ireland (a division of Penguin Books Ltd).
Penguin Group (Australia), 250 Camberwell Road, Camberwell, Victoria 3124, Australia (a division of Pearson
Australia Group Pty Ltd). Penguin Books India Pvt Ltd, 11 Community Centre, Panchsheel Park,
New Delhi - 110 017, India. Penguin Group (NZ), 67 Apollo Drive, Rosedale, Auckland 0632,
New Zealand (a division of Pearson New Zealand Ltd). Penguin Books (South Africa) (Pty) Ltd, 24 Sturdee
Avenue, Rosebank, Johannesburg 2196, South Africa. Penguin Books Ltd, Registered Offices:
80 Strand, London WC2R 0RL, England.

Design by Amy Wu. Text set in 14-point Adobe Caslon. The illustrations are rendered in pencils and markers.

Library of Congress Cataloging-in-Publication Data
Polacco, Patricia. Bully / Patricia Polacco. p. cm.
Summary: Sixth-grade friends Lyla and Jamie, both new to their school,
stand up for each other when a clique of popular girls bullies them online.
[1. Friendship—Fiction. 2. Cyberbullying—Fiction.
3. Bullies—Fiction. 4. Popularity—Fiction. 5. Schools—Fiction.] I. Title.
PZ7.P75186Bul 2012 [Fic]—dc23 2011046777

ISBN 978-0-399-25704-9
1 3 5 7 9 10 8 6 4 2